I0640957

Firebrand Firestorm

The Ancestors of Bjorn Esterday

Volume 09

Onward

May & June 1776

Wynter Sommers

Wynter Sommers

Published by Pure Force Enterprises, Inc.
California, USA
Since 2002

INGRAM

INGRAM® Distribution

ISBN-13: 978-1-7184-0021-4
ISBN-10: 1-7184-0021-7

DEDICATION

To those who feel strongly about truth, justice, and the integrity of America; your honorable actions make us proud. To those who wonder if their daily choices matter; your small decisions impact generations to come. To those everyday people who don't think they have what it takes; when you strive for extraordinary things, the impossible becomes reality. Your dreams today become our future tomorrow.Thank you for everything you do.

Bjorn Esterday
Was Not Born Yesterday
Series

Firebrand (15 Volumes+Conversation Station Book)
Edges (9 Stories +Conversation Station Book)
Gone (18 Stories + Conversation Station Book)

Bjorn EDGES Series

EDGES Book 1-Swift Encounter
EDGES Book 2-Rousing Attack
EDGES Book 3-One Foot Under
EDGES Book 4-Earthshake
EDGES Book 5-Broken String
EDGES Book 6-Key Witness
EDGES Book 7-Who is She?
EDGES Book 8-Vanish
EDGES Book 9-Chase or Die

Bjorn Series Alternate Reading Plan

1st	Edges Book 1		22nd	Gone Book 10
2nd	Edges Book 2		23rd	Firebrand Vol 9
3rd	Gone Book 1		24rd	Gone Book 11
4th	Firebrand Vol 1		25th	Firebrand Vol 10
5th	Edges Book 3		26th	Gone Book 12
6th	Firebrand Vol 2		27th	Gone Book 13
7th	Gone Book 2		28th	Firebrand Vol 11
8th	Gone Book 3		29th	Gone Book 14
9th	Firebrand Vol 3		30th	Firebrand Vol 12
10th	Gone Book 4		31st	Gone Book 15
11th	Firebrand Vol 4		32nd	Firebrand Vol 13
12th	Gone Book 5		33rd	Gone Book 16
13th	Gone Book 6		34th	Firebrand Vol 14
14th	Edges Book 4		35th	Gone Book 17
15th	Firebrand Vol 5		36th	Firebrand Vol15 (End)
16th	Gone Book 7		37th	Gone Book 18 (End)
17th	Firebrand Vol 6		38th	Edges Book 5
18th	Gone Book 8		39th	Edges Book 6
19th	Firebrand Vol 7		40th	Edges Book 7
20th	Gone Book 9		41st	Edges Book 8
21st	Firebrand Vol 8		42nd	Edges Book 9(End)

ACKNOWLEDGMENTS

We acknowledge those who actively build peace. We acknowledge all the selfless talent which contributed to creating meaningful tokens of consideration and sharing. We acknowledge that every person has a daily choice of right or wrong... and we thank you for choosing the right, good, honorable path filled with integrity because that is the difficult and brave path. Small choices today become lasting monuments of loving hope tomorrow

CONTENTS

0 PREFACE

Mrs. Dunlap, Polly, TallMan and his mother, Eunice, have all been sharing stories about captivity. They reveal how it was possible to navigate oppressive situations to stay alive, and then take tragedy and use it to propel them to do good for others.

TallMan quietly disclosed that when his beloved intended bride died, he left his people and went out into the world to learn medicine from other cultures and is now ready to return to Canada to bring healing and life and to cure those ailments which had brought death to his people.

1 CHAPTER 81: (JUNE 1776) Mrs. Dunlap Gets a Letter

Gentle morning light streamed into the dining room of the printer's house. Mr. John Dunlap bade his wife farewell, mounted his steed, and prepared to ride off to his print shop in town.

"Good that Polly," Mr. Dunlap shared with his wife as he shoved a letter into her hand, "knows German. I'm off to meet with Henrich Millers to consult about printing something up. Read this to Polly, my dear, would you?"

Mrs. Dunlap accepted the letter and waved to her husband as he galloped away.

Mrs. Dunlap walked back inside and returned to the dining hall. Immediately, she walked to the sideboard and placed a strip of crispy bacoun onto her plate before rejoining Polly, now great with child, seated at the breakfast table.

"What is that in your hand, Mrs. Dunlap?" Polly asked as she sipped a cup of hot tea.

"Oh! That darling husband of mine. Well, Mr. Dunlap said a messenger had just arrived with this letter. He said I should read it to you. Then, off he galloped to work," Mrs. Dunlap sighed, "I'm still so very in love with my husband, Polly. 'Tis a blessing after all these years."

Simms, the Dunlap's family butler, opened the dining room door to allow a footman, holding a hot fresh platter of eggs and crispy squares of bacoun. Simms held the door open while the footman replaced the empty tray with fresh hot food on the sideboard. The footman then took his place, standing at attention, while Simms left to inspect the rest of the household.

"Who wrote the letter?" Polly asked Mrs. Dunlap.

"Oh, it is from Mr. Robert Livingston," Mrs. Dunlap replied expecting Polly to recall the name. Polly did not.

"I have mentioned him before, Polly," Mrs. Dunlap pouted.

Polly shook her head, "I am so sorry, Mrs. Dunlap. I simply do not recall any details about a Mr. Livingston."

"Well," Mrs. Dunlap started as the footman refilled her tea cup with piping hot water poured over a silver strainer. He tapped the strainer to catch loose tea leaves which had been steeping in the teapot. The footman then stepped back and resumed his unobtrusive position awaiting to fulfill the next order.

"Yes?" Polly prompted.

"Robert Livingston," Mrs. Dunlap explained, "...is a man of fine penmanship, but he suffers from doubts. Oft times, he refuses to write unless he has a fully perfect and complete letter in his mind's eye, but recently he has been unable to write a thing because there is no clear goal established in the meetings he has been attending."

Polly inquired, "Meetings? Of what nature are these meetings?"

"In the past," Mrs. Dunlap said, "He has penned letters to officials to address various topics of concern in the Colonies."

Mrs, Dunlap looked up to be quite certain that she had Polly's full attention before she continued, "He is the son of two very wealthy Hudson River Valley families, you see. Educated at King's College in '64. He's just formed an unofficial group he calls the Committee of Five. It says here the others all agreed on June 11th. Very recent indeed."

"What is the purpose of that committee?" Polly asked.

"Oh, I am not entirely certain, Polly." Mrs. Dunlap shook her head, "But I believe it has something to do with asking His Majesty to leave the Colonies be."

"That is a bold request, is it not, Mrs. Dunlap?" Polly commented.

"Well," Mrs. Dunlap shook her head, "Those boys think they can make a difference. Many have tried before, you know."

"Boys?" Polly asked.

"The five. The Committee," Mrs. Dunlap smiled. She held up her hand and pointed to each finger as she rattled off names, "John Adams, Benjamin Franklin, Roger Sherman, Thomas Jefferson, and of course Robert Livingston. Five."

"And what does his letter say?" Polly asked.

"Oh! Indeed," Mrs. Dunlap realized she had drifted somewhat off topic and glanced at the letter, then laid it on the table before she continued, "There might be agreement amongst the colonies. A unification. Mr. Livingston feels inspired to draft a letter, which will force His Majesty to respond. At least, they hope for a reply."

Polly recalled, "Not only was Jane gracious enough to bring me to your home, but she is also trying to complete the task her Uncle Floyd started before he died. She told me he wanted to stop the raids on colonist homes and halt the kidnappings to sell us as slaves. Do you think that sort of change could take place?"

"Change is usually brief..." Mrs. Dunlap shared, "Perhaps we can hope for a year or two?"

"A year of peace would be most welcomed." Polly concurred, "Pity peace could not last longer."

"A year of freedom from his Majesty's distant management is better than no change at all," Mrs. Dunlap encouraged

"Yes," Polly agreed and bit off a square piece of crispy bacoun.

"Every person who has endured that horrid journey to this land left some manner of oppression behind. They came here for a better life. They did not ask to be snatched from their homes to be made slaves. They did not ask to work diligently to amass lands only to sell them when His Majesty needed money.

They did not ask for their sons to be whisked into the King's navy against their will..." Mrs. Dunlap sighed, "Hannah Duston was raided a century ago. *Eunice Williams Marguerite Kanenstenhawi Arosen* was raided half a century ago... and you mere months ago."

"Fortunately for Eunice, the tribe which took her in learned the love of Christ and treated her like family," Polly noted.

"And you, Polly. You were raided only a few months ago and lived." Mrs. Dunlap commented, "God's providence allowed Jane Hargreaves to employ Billy Dawes as a driver. Otherwise, you might have died at the side of the road instead of being brought here."

Polly replied, "I am thankful for all that."

"Only God could arrange such events," Mrs. Dunlap reminded Polly. "Even the events which disrupt our placid lives can lead to something. Since the 1400's... for three centuries people have left civilized cities, endured a harsh journey, and embraced the wilderness of this land, but now our new hurdle is to demand respect from the throne."

"Constant struggles are exhausting when you don't see an end to them," Polly commented. "Perhaps Mr. Livingston was simply discouraged by the fact that the throne has more power, weapons, organized militia, and we... we are but common folk. It is a battle lost before it is even fought."

"Not a single soul wants to fight His Majesty. Not a single woman wants to lose another husband, as you did, Polly. Nay, they wish to settle the matter with negotiations instead. But if forced, we must prove we mean the terms we draft, as a unified body. We must stand fast to our consistent ideal," Mrs.Dunlap replied.

"So, will Mr. Livingston write the letter to King George?" Polly asked.

Mrs. Dunlap mused, "He writes... now let me see, here..." Mrs. Dunlap skimmed the letter, then looked at Polly with a smile, "Robert Livingston met an outspoken servant at the last meeting. The fellow was well spoken and able to articulate clearly to the crowd. Mr. Livingston says this servant ignited a fiery integrity of purpose in the crowd. And..." Mrs. Dunlap smiled broadly, "Mr. Livingston has penned the first few sentences."

"Oh," Polly said, "Good thing Mr. Livingston was inspired by that servant... Good news, that."

"Yes it is, Polly! Very good news..." Mrs. Dunlap smiled, "I'd like to meet that servant and thank him, one day." Mrs. Dunlap nodded to herself.

"Oh, Mrs. Dunlap," Polly started, "I told Mr. Dunlap that I would translate the document... Into German so everybody could read the terms. Does Mr. Livingston include enough for me to start translating?"

Mrs. Dunlap pushed back her chair. With a glance, she notified the footman, who was standing by, to help Polly as she tried to stand. He did. Mrs. Dunlap motioned Polly to follow her. They walked into the library where there was a writing desk. Mrs. Dunlap indicated that Polly should sit.

"Yes, Polly," Mrs. Dunlap started, "I think Mr. Livingston included enough to start a translation. Mrs. Dunlap glanced about. "The question is... what shall you write it on?"

Polly looked around and saw the vellum her husband had purchased at the general store before their cabin was raided. This was the one memory of her husband she clung to as she desperately escaped from both the Indians and the wild boar Polly had encountered in the woods. This was the same parchment Silversmith had gotten repaired for her. It was rolled up with a large ribbon around it, propped up on the writing desk.

Polly replied, "I believe we should assume Mr. Livingston's words will last for more than a year. I would like to pen the German translation on the Vellum Button Gwinette purchased at the General Store before we were raided."

Mrs. Dunlap placed a hand on Polly's shoulder and said, "That is a loving sacrificial gesture which will honor the death of your husband, Polly. I know you said he wanted to use it to explain to your first born how you two met and fell in love."

Polly reached up for a German dictionary and a sheet of common paper, "I shall endeavor to have as fine a hand as Robert Livingston. I will practice on these pages first, then I shall write the final German draft on my husband's vellum, which he purchased because he said it would last. He said he would document how he and I fell in love to act as firm instructions to our first born on making wise choices in life..."

Polly's eyes welled with tears. She inhaled slowly, and placed the common paper flat on the writing table in front of her. Then she smoothed the page from

Robert Livingston's letter, which had the start of his formal document.

She slid the ink well near her, and the blotter. Deliberately, she took the quill in her hand and slowly dipped it into the inkwell, lightly tapping off the excess droplets of ink before touching the nib to the sheet.

"I can procure a fresh vellum, Polly. You don't need to use the one your husband gave to you..." Mrs. Dunlap soothed.

Then Polly paused and looked at Mrs. Dunlap, "I would rather honor the memory of my husband by telling my first born that this vellum contributed to the edification of freedom in the colonies."

Mrs. Dunlap nodded briefly, "There are so many German speakers who do not know English, Polly. Your translation will inform a great many people my husband's English words could never reach... But are you sure you want to use that particular vellum?"

Polly smiled and replied, "By using Button's vellum, it will help me forget the attack on my home. And if I can tell my firstborn child that Button's vellum allowed our German speaking population to know they were free... that Button contributed to that peace and our freedom posthumously... it would mean a great deal..."

Polly reached for the vellum with the ribbon around it and touched it lightly, "I have decided, Mrs. Dunlap, when I get the translation just right, I'll pen it directly on this..." she looked at Mrs. Dunlap and smiled.

"I'm sure," Mrs. Dunlap said softly, "That Mr. Livingston has the best penmanship of that Committee of Five. I believe Thomas Jefferson has the finest words of them all. Although they are still developing the letter to the King, Robert Livingston will send us a faithful copy of those words to my husband. Then I shall give it to you to translate."

"But how will this translation get to the German speakers?" Polly asked.

Mrs. Dunlap smiled at Polly and replied, "I can ask Mr. Dunlap to get Henrich Millers to print it up and distribute it to the German speaking colonists. Know this Polly, that with your German translation of Robert Livingston's letter on the King's desk, all colonists will comprehend the gravity of change we are about to undertake... and your husband's vellum contribution will also be well-remembered. Now, Polly, let us hear how Mr. Jefferson's words sound in Robert Livingston's hand writing? Please read aloud the first sentence..."

Polly set down her quill and held up the letter from Robert Livingston. She read, "The unanimous Declaration of the thirteen united States of America... When in the Course of human events, it becomes necessary for one people to dissolve the political bands which have connected them..."

"Dissolve from King George? Permanently?" Mrs. Dunlap giggled with a clasp of her hands, "I sense a royal storm brewing... I'll leave you to it, Polly"

Mrs. Dunlap left the room and overheard Polly murmuring to herself, then the scratch of the quill nib to paper as Polly worked out her thoughts.

Fading away, as Mrs. Dunlap walked down the hall, she could hear Polly speaking aloud in German:

"Wenn es im Lauf menschlicher Gegebenheiten für ein Volk nöthig wird die Politische Bande, wodurch es mit einem andern verknüpft gewesen, zu trennen, und unter den Mächten der Erden...."

2 CHAPTER 82: (JUNE 1776)
Silversmith Sees Stable Boys
Returning too Fast.

The barn was now becoming a mere shadow as the afternoon faded to evening. All stable boys had been instructed by Susanna Wright to keep the horses in pasture as long as possible, to allow the meeting to take place in the barn. The winds were picking up and the stable boys knew they had to return to get the horses into their stalls. Over the knoll, the boys led the horses slowly back toward the barn with simple ropes.

Silversmith, still hiding behind the haystack, saw them on the horizon and knew her time was limited. Could she manage to return to where Billy Dawes and Peter Timothy were waiting for her in the carriage at the edge of the corn field?

Could Silversmith dash from hay stack to hay stack without being noticed, now that one of the men she was listening to is aware of a sound and now intent on investigating the noise? Did the noise, which Silversmith herself had made, accidentally revealing her location?

Silversmith estimated she had about ten minutes before the stable boys noticed her. Would they betray her location or bring attention to her?

Would Henry Mossop's men, the ones looking for white slaves to sell, simply catch her and add her to their inventory by forcing her aboard a ship to a foreign land from which there would be no escape?

Rustling now emanated from within the barn, drawing the attentions of the men back toward the large doors of the barn.

The door jiggled as if the crowd inside were ready to disburse.

Perhaps a speaker was uttering closing comments before excusing the attendees. But, then the door remained silent and Silversmith dreaded that the men would resume their investigation to find the source of the noise which Silversmith had made.

She could not run without being seen, and she was quite confident that these men could overtake her in a foot pursuit.

She had to think.

She could not allow these men to know she had overheard their conversation.

At least one and probably two would recognize her and that would jeopardize... well... everyone.

The men would know she was sent by Jane and that would put Jane in danger. On her first assignment, the first time Miss Jane had entrusted her with something really important... she was about to be the cause of its failure.

Then, in the distance, on the horizon, Silversmith saw one of the stable boys mount the horse he was leading.

He was going to ride the horse back to the barn, which meant it would come sooner than she had previously estimated.

No longer did she have ten luxurious minutes. Now, she had half that time to try and escape undetected.

One by one, the other stable boys followed suit and also mounted their horses. Silversmith tried to spy the carriage in the distance, but it was now too dark to see where it was.

If she could not see the carriage, then Billy Dawes and his spyglass could not see her.

She was alone.

"No!" Silversmith thought silently to herself. "The stable boys are returning too soon". Henry Mossop's men were now stepping closer. She could hear their boots crunch across the dirt as they moved.

3 CHAPTER 83: (JUNE 1776) Where is Jane?

As Mrs. Dunlap walked down the hallway, leaving Polly to translate the letter from Robert Livingston into German, she heard a quiet knock at the front door. Mrs. Dunlap was preoccupied with thoughts of the future. Could the colonial States of British America really become united?

Simms, the Dunlap butler, quickly sped to the door and when he saw Mrs. Dunlap, he paused to say, "That is messenger boy who came right when you bade farewell to the Colonist lady and her Indian son..."

"Eunice and TallMan, yes, Simms... What did the messenger's note say?" Mrs. Dunlap asked.

Simms the Butler replied, "It said there was a man looking for Jane Hargreaves and he may come by..."

"And you neglected to tell me?" Mrs. Dunlap put one hand on her hip.

Simms replied, "I did notify Mr. Dunlap, but since there was no specific date mentioned, I did not wish to burden you, Mrs. Dunlap. It was an error in judgment on my part and I apologize."

The knocker on the door rapped once more. The visitor must be getting impatient.

"Oh, Mr. Dunlap has become so forgetful these days. Pay no attention to it, Simms. I cannot be bothered with trivialities. But, if that impatient creature at the door has word of Jane Hargreaves, I would suggest you answer it... and I shall receive him. If it is not to do with Miss Hargreaves, then send him away and Polly and I will take tea in the library. I will now warn Polly we might be getting a visitor and if not, tea. Either way, please let us know what is afoot, Simms."

Simms acknowledged the direction of his mistress and went to the front door as Mrs. Dunlap returned to the library to notify Polly.

Just as Polly and Mrs. Dunlap situated themselves on the sofa in the library, Simms entered the room and announced, "Mr. Bryce Aiden Tyler, Madame."

"Thank you, Simms." Mrs. Dunlap dismissed him and welcomed this new visitor, "Mr. Tyler, is it? I believe we received a cryptic note saying you are acquainted with..." Mrs. Dunlap hesitated, forcing the visitor to finish her sentence.

Bryce Aiden Tyler replied, "I am... was the business partner to Floyd Hargreaves, Jane Hargreaves' deceased uncle. Through correspondence from Miss Hargreaves lady's maid to Floyd Hargreaves' butler, it has come to my attention that you, Mrs. Dunlap, are acqainted with Miss Hargreaves."

"Indeed I am, Mr. Tyler. Won't you sit down?" Mrs. Dunlap offered, "May I introduce Polly Mulhoolin. Miss Mulhoolin is also a friend of Miss Hargreaves. Please do tell me the nature of your visit..."

"I realize, " Bryce Aiden Tyler started, "that this is most unusual. One could interpret my intrusion as rude, but I assure you I am desperately seeking answers and would not have interrupted your day unless I felt it quite necessary."

"Is Jane in any trouble?" Polly asked.

"Well, I've just come from," Bryce Aiden Tyler started, "...from Sarah Wilson's estate and it appears Miss Hargreaves has gone missing... as has her Lady's Maid, Silversmith."

"Pardon?" Mrs. Dunlap exclaimed.

Bryce Aiden Tyler impatiently spoke somewhat louder, "Witherspoon, the butler at the Hargreaves residence, and I suspect she may be in danger... Pardon my direct questioning, but has Jane Hargreaves come here?"

"She has visited me several times," Polly shared, "But not recently."

"Are you quite certain she is missing, Mr. Tyler? Perhaps she has taken a few days to shop, or order a dress to be designed..." Mrs. Dunlap offered, "If I may say so, Mr. Tyler, you appear to be exhausted from a long and tedious journey. Perhaps your judgment is... compromised?"

"I assure you," Bryce replied, "My judgment is quite sound. I am concerned for Miss Hargreaves' safety. According to Lady Sarah Wilson…"

"Oh, she is not a genuine 'Lady'. The woman actually gave herself that title, and she didn't even have the sense to name herself after an earldom. Imagine!" Mrs. Dunlap informed her visitor.

"Self-titled or not," Bryce continued, "A person posing as the titled Lady of the Sarah Wilson estate…'

"Oh," Mrs. Dunlap interjected, "and it's not her estate, but a discarded property from one of her ex- lovers who has left and returned to Europe."

Bryce Aiden persisted, "She said Silversmith… do you know her? She is Jane Hargreaves' maid. According to slaves at Lady Sarah Wilson's estate, Silversmith left days before Jane did."

"Why would a maid leave ahead of her mistress?" Mrs. Dunlap asked.

"That is what I am trying to discover," Bryce Aiden Tyler stated as he continued, "They were told that Silversmith returned home with the driver, a Mr. Billy Dawes, but neither Silversmith nor Mr. Dawes has returned. I have verified this with the Hargreaves butler, Witherspoon."

"Perhaps Jane has taken a shopping trip for a day or so... to get some lace made, perhaps?" Polly offered.

Bryce Aiden shook his head, "I do not think she would indulge in such a frivolity knowing her purpose for being at the estate in the first place was to evaluate matters pertaining to her Uncle Floyd. And if she did choose to travel, would she not need her carriage driver for such a journey? No. In fact, her personal items were still at the estate."

"Has the butler heard from any of them?" Mrs. Dunlap asked.

"I am afraid," Bryce explained, "Witherspoon has not received a single word from Silversmith, nor the carriage driver Billy Dawes, nor Jane Hargreaves. This is vexing. I am searching for Miss Hargreaves and have brought Magistrate Karl Pinkney with me. He awaits for me in the carriage outside."

"Well, I can send word," Mrs. Dunlap offered, "To have Jane's things sent back to her Uncle's home. That is a simple matter."

"Mrs. Dunlap," Bryce Aiden Tyler, trying not to lose his patience, reinforced, "It is not Jane's things... Miss Hargreaves' personal luggage I am concerned about... it is her very person. Do you know or do your servants know where she or Silversmith may have gone?"

Both Polly Mulhoolin and Mrs. Dunlap shook their heads. Nobody knew where Jane had vanished.

4 CHAPTER 84: (JUNE 1776) Button at the end of the Barn meeting

Inside the barn, the assembled crowd discussed Henry Mossop's proclamation of doom should they unify and ask the King of England to leave all thirteen colonies be.

As the murmuring subsided, Button abruptly spoke up, "I have never been one with strong opinions, but I can discern that Mr. Mossop's penchant for the drama of an operatic performance, seems to justify in his mind, that he can treat his neighbor in any manner he chooses. I assume, he also feels he should never suffer consequences if he treats his fellow man unjustly. I do not think we can take the threats of a man like that seriously."

Farmer gave Button a stern look as if to caution him to be silent. Looking away from Farmer, Button noticed a man fiddling with the latch on the barn door.

"You there..." Button announced.

The man replied, "The stable boys are returning. It is time for our meeting to adjourn. We have come to no agreement just as in our last meeting. A storm may be approaching and we should all return to warm beds and hot suppers."

Button challenged a retort, "Because of weather, do you, sir, condone the actions of men who thirst for power, abuse it, and justify enslaving us simply because we are alive? Have the hardships foisted on me and my... presumably dead wife... been for naught?"

The man stopped fiddling with the barn door and stepped back into the crowd, murmuring, "As Mr. Mossop said, it is our lot. We cannot survive on this island without the king. We must accept that this land will be governed as Europe is."

A man named Adams commented, "Checks and balances must be put into place. Human nature can never be trusted with absolute power. "

"If North America were united," Button started as a strong gust of wind whistled through the planks of the barn, "we should stop conducting business with any group, which hinders unification of all colonies."

"Stop trading with them?" The crowd demanded as if calculating the cost of lost business.

Benjamin Franklin stepped in, "Indeed, this Button fellow speaks as a true Son of Liberty. If certain businesses wish to remain in bondage to their royalist concepts, let them. But any business wishing to secure me as a customer should actively support unification of the Colonies. I urge you all to never frequent supporters of the King. Do not walk into their shops, nor reward them with your repeated business. If they do not wish to be free, that is their choice."

Thomas Jefferson immediately added, "But I never shop. It is my servants or slaves who shop for me. I cannot control their loyalties, nor which shops they frequent."

Benjamin Franklin replied, "For any who employ indentured servants from Germany, you may find some of them recall that George the third had Germanic heritage and, therefore, they will remain loyal to the English King! But not all of them think this way. And yes, we have all succumbed to buying slaves. I believe, you, Mr. Jefferson actually own quite a few. But in this new land, there shall be new rules."

"Yes," Mr. Jefferson concurred. "When I married my wife, her dowry had over 100 slaves. I also purchased them for my estate. I felt that the estate simply could not run without that many people to keep the day to day operations smooth." He turned to Samuel Adams and pointed, "But, you, Mr.Adams, have received a slave as a gift!"

Mr. Adams frowned at Mr. Jefferson as he replied, "Indeed, back in 1765 I was given Surry. I do want you to note, however, that I freed her as a slave and offered her payment if she willingly chose to remain our family cook. She appears to be happy with this arrangement because to this day, Surry is still in my employ. Even if I want slavery to be outlawed in my Massachusetts, it means nothing until all the colonies agree to banish slavery. You will notice that once any person is valued for their skills and compensated with fair wages, you actually get better work out of them.

Fewer mistakes..."

Button asked, "So you are saying it actually costs you less to value your workers, give them salary, so they willingly contribute? I see you have discovered that demanding anything of resentful slaves will simply cause them to execute tasks slowly and even hinder any progress by purposely misunderstanding requests or worse. This will eventually cost more. I have seen it in the slaves of my employer in Georgia."

Mr. Samuel Adams nodded.

Thomas Jefferson scoffed, "Slavery supports commerce. There is no negative argument for it."

Samuel Adams snapped back, "When my cousin John spoke before Continental Congress earlier this year, he refused to omit from the trade resolutions a particular argument. He stated that NO slaves shall be imported into any of our thirteen colonies. John and I foresee our nation as being free from all slavery. No person should work without fair wages in exchange for their labors."

The crowd reacted with elevated noisy conversation.

Mr. Adams shook his head as he scanned the crowd saying, "My cousin John and I have discussed that if slavery remains in our country.... We anticipate calamity and friction, not unity. In private, he tells me slavery is akin to gangrene, which must be stopped! One day, he will be confident to pronounce his thoughts publicly."

The crowd continued to buzz with excitement.

"I, sirs and madams," Button started, "ask you to place yourselves in my position. I was wrested from my home. Why? It now appears that I was one of many Colonists who are snatched from their homes to be sold as slaves. Perhaps it is lucrative. Perhaps it is because I was not an active supporter of the King. Perhaps it was because my wife was Irish, a race hated by the English. I know not the reason, but it happened to me and it can happen to you, next. Did not all of us come to this land, willing to endure the hardships because we hunger for the liberties this country offers? Why then do we so easily surrender our freedoms to the rule of one country or another? Why can we not unify and rule ourselves? Is it not worth it to fight to maintain our freedom?"

One man shouted above the murmur of the crowd, "Eliminating business transactions with Royalists is a goodly sum of business. If we are to stop doing business with them, that is a very great financial sacrifice... Even now, if we do not vacate this barn, we may all be punished by his majesty's guards. I wish to go home and hide."

"Sir," Mr. Samuel Adams stated, "I ask you this. Is it wrong to meet to discuss a topic? The king you fear is in England... across the ocean. Why does he have the power to arrest people who meet in a barn?"

Adams continued, "Perhaps what you should wish for is the freedom of speech. Perhaps you should consider if that freedom is worth the temporary cessation of using tea, wine, molasses, syrups, panels, coffee, sugar, pimento, indigo dyes and inks, foreign paper, glass, and painters' colors? "

"Who gives his Majesty the right," Button shouted at the crowd, "to allow the enslavement of Colonial residents to be a profitable and legitimate business? Is it acceptable to each person here to go home and find a member of your family missing because the King has decided to sell one member of your family as a slave? I owed no debts. I was not rebellious against the king. Why was I taken from inside my own cabin? "

A woman shouted from the crowd. "I heard there is a magistrate in another town with a brother who had to pay gold to the throne for a crime. He sold everything, is still paying, and still does not know what crime he committed."

Button continued, "Is it justice for the monarch of England to demand financial restitution for a crime here in the British American colonies, but to never name the nature of the crime? Is it enough to receive a document which says a trial was held on your behalf in England and you were found guilty and you need not have been present at the trial?"

Samuel Adams added, "Perhaps you should wish for the ability to make a law which states you should know which crime you are accused of and you will have a trial in the presence of the accused."

A doubter charged, "You believe all criminals should be free, then?"

"Nay," Button retorted, "Crime should be punished. It is my thought that all crimes should be thoroughly investigated. If the evidence indicates a specific culprit, then that person should be given a trial by his peers in front of an impartial judge. I have seen men arrested and neither the soldiers arresting, nor the man being arrested, knows the nature of these criminal charges. Such orders are signed en mass in England and not investigated. It is possible an official of the crown can be guilty of negligence or malfeasance, either of which could mistakenly accuse an innocent person and let the guilty go free. Neither of which is just."

Robert Livingston echoed, "He that justifieth the wicked, and he that condemneth the just, even they both are abominations to the Lord. That is in the seventeenth book of Proverbs, the fifteenth verse."

"You sir," one man from the crowd challenged Button directly, "are merely echoing what Peyton Randolph documented two years ago in October 1774. His letter did not unify any of us. It changed nothing. Why should penning a new document be any different?"

"Perhaps," Robert Livingston suggested, "Instead of giving up, we should improve upon Randolph's document. We need to improve on the obsequious letter written last year, July 8th 1775 , when we asked his Most Gracious Sovereign to review our humble petition. Perhaps we should not be so humble," Livingston folded his arms.

Mr. Samuel Adams stated, "If we unite and write a letter to His Majesty, it must be dated before July the 8th otherwise he will remember the anniversary of Peyton Randolph's failed letter. "

The crowd agreed, but one could hear some groaning as if they would not assist and others trying to convince them otherwise. The noise rose until Mr. Adams spoke over the crowd.

Samuel Adams said, "Each and every one of us must participate in the terms Mr. Livingston will write." Adams looked each man in the eye as he pointed at a person and called out the colony they were from, "I will represent

Massachusetts bay. You, sir, are from New Hampshire. You are from Rhode Island and you there... back there from Providence Plantations. I see men from Connecticut, New York, New Jersey, Pennsylvania. Is there a man from one of the counties of New Castle, Kent, and Sussex on Delaware?

Ah, yes. I see you. And over there is a man from Maryland. You, Sir, are from Virginia. And you over there are from North Carolina standing next to the fellow from South Carolina."

Button invigorated with enthusiasm asked, "What of Savannah, Georgia? I realize Georgia is south of the Carolina Colonies, but it can have a voice as its own colony. I have a parcel of land in Georgia. It is currently being looked after by a friend. I could gather a militia and push even further south to take over the Florida peninsula to enlarge Georgia's Colonial border. Could I also be a voice, representing Georgia in your document of unification?"

Mr. Adams looked at the crowd and turned to Button, speaking loudly so the whole barn could hear, "Mr. Button, you are welcomed to participate as a voice of unifying the Colonies." He turned to the crowd, "Unifying means we make our own laws. We manufacture products here and no longer import. We price our goods so we can afford to buy what we make."

Thomas Jefferson interrupted, "I agree with your perspective on commerce, but are you quite certain it is imperative for us all to release our slaves... or start paying them as if they were servants?"

Mr. Hancock looked sharply at Thomas Jefferson, "What do you fear will happen, Mr. Jefferson?"

Mr. Jefferson took a deep breath and replied, "Mr. Hancock, I have an obligation to provide food and shelter to my slaves as I have a vast estate. In exchange for food and shelter, my slaves tend to my estate, keeping it in working order and provide... other services which

I fear I cannot live without." He turned to Mr. Adams. "Mr.Adams. Sir. Must we all live without our slaves and reduce our quality of circumstances? I do not see how my living without slaves would make King George suddenly leave all thirteen colonies alone to govern themselves."

Samuel Adams frowned at Thomas Jefferson, "Consider this. You have commented that the King of England is treating you... and the rest of us... as slaves unable to own anything. Would it not be a fitting gesture to ask King George to free us as we also free our own slaves?"

"But," Mr. Jefferson persisted, "How could one run a society without slaves?"

Mr. Adams replied, "I propose a new economy. One which pays all workers. One which encourages innovations and inventions as our own Mr. Franklin has demonstrated. I propose factory workers should be able to earn the products they manufacture. I propose a standard of quality all Colonies agree to. If we are united in these things, if we eschew barbaric tactics and approach King George as civilized gentlemen, he cannot ignore us."

"How would you," Button asked Robert Livingston, "write a letter so it does not seem rebellious and treasonous?"

Mr. Livingston looked at Samuel Adams and said, "We should remind his Majesty that we have been faithful to his crown."

Samuel Adams added, " We have done so despite the abuse our families have endured without cause. We have been true to England even when his Majesty's seemingly capricious ministers and soldiers randomly carry out orders which make no sense and are probably an error."

Mr. Livingston continued, "Then, we can firmly, yet kindly, request all thirteen colonies be left alone. There are many issues we can address. Each man here is flawed and has been guilty of one matter or another in the past, but what our goal should be is to strive for a better future, a united future. Now, in that unified spirit, I can pen words to let His Majesty know that we will not be swayed by any brutal tactics. We must peacefully resolve to be... to be..."

Mr. Adams assisted Mr. Livingston in finding the right words, "To be an independent state within these British American Colonies."

Mr. Hancock looked around, then asked the participants, "Who in this room is in agreement?"

5 CHAPTER 85: (JUNE 1776) Jane's Carriage trip

A while before Bryce Aiden Tyler and Magistrate Karl Pinkney had embarked on a hunt for Jane Hargreaves, Jane had been making quiet travel plans of her own.

Instead of alerting the slaves at the Wilson estate, Jane walked to town one early morning, carrying only her small carpet bag. She left quietly, knowing the stroll into town would take quite a long time by foot. She had closed the door to her room and hoped she would be back by dinner before Lady Sarah Wilson might notice she was missing.

Her goal was to ride to meeting town; meet whomever Silversmith and Billy Dawes had found; pay off any extra bills at the inn where Silversmith and Billy Dawes were lodging;, and then have Billy Dawes drive the carriage back to the estate, collect her things and head home.

A very simple plan, indeed.

She was relieved when she finally had arrived at the village and saw the carriage station.

She noted the sign on the tavern, which was near the row of tethered horses. There was a picture of a rising sun on that sign. Jane overheard a passerby mentioning Summer Hill had the best tavern in all Cecil County of Maryland.

A bit tired and with sore feet, Jane took a deep breath, inhaling to resettle her torso within her corset. She set down her carpet bag, and placed her hands on her hips as the cool morning air wafted around her arms which she held akimbo, providing refreshing relief from the warmth which the walk had generated.

Jane picked up her carpet bag and, striding the remaining few steps to the carriage station, she stopped before a uniformed ticket man.

"Is this Nottingham Lot Seventeen? Does this carriage head north to the Meeting Town?" Jane asked the uniformed man securing passengers for the hired carriages.

"Madame, our carriages can be hired to travel north all the way to the Canadian border, if you can pay for it." The ticket man noticed Jane's perplexed reaction and further explained, "The Meeting Town is for more politically minded folk."

"You know how to get to Meeting Town?" Jane clarified.

He leaned in very close to Jane and said, "Meeting Town is a code. You mustn't say it too loudly. It changes location each meeting. So, Meeting Town is constantly moving. 'Tis only for those who... don't fully endorse the actions of the King of England."

Jane leaned in and whispered, "I was written and instructed to go there today. Would you take me north or south of Summer Hill's Rising Sun?"

"Our carriage can take you all the way to the Canadian border, but I would suggest heading north and stop in Philadelphia. Then I would ask your contacts where you must go from there."

Jane smiled, now understanding, set down her carpet bag and reached into her skirt pocket, extracting a coin.

Jane said, "I'd like to leave immediately, please." She indicated the carriage nearby, where a boy was brushing down the horses and another boy was checking to make sure the carriage was properly secured to the horses.

The ticket man replied, "There are two other passengers who have already purchased a ticket to Canada. They have stepped away, but should return shortly."

"I am to share a carriage?" Jane asked, unused to this custom of a public carriage, having lived a very different life in England before her fortunes were reallocated to a distant cousin. She asked, "Is there sufficient room inside the carriage for three?"

"Oh, it will hold six tightly, if need be," the carriage man reassured.

"Could I," Jane asked, "purchase passage to Meeting Town and return this very night before supper?"

"Hmmm..." The carriage man rubbed his chin, "Our other carriage is due here shortly, but is scheduled to head south. It is already full with other passengers. You are heading north. So, I'm afraid you may need to spend a night or two in Philadelphia. After our Canadian passengers are deposited at the border, we can arrange for our driver to collect you later from meeting town and return you here."

"Oh, I was not planning on spending a night or two..." Jane mused, "I simply wanted to know. I have arranged to have a private carriage waiting for me... but I wanted to know what other options might be available. Simply gathering information, you see."

"Do you," The carriage man started, "...still want to purchase passage to Meeting Town, or would you rather return in a few days to secure private passage to and from Meeting Town in one day... assuming the location remains the same?"

"No. No... If you have room on the carriage and if it can get me there tonight, I will purchase the ticket. People are expecting me to arrive... so..." Jane commented. She then finished purchasing her ticket from the carriage man.

The man gave her a small paper receipt and said, "Show this to the driver so he knows you are heading North, Ma'am. You can take a seat over there while you wait. There might be other passengers who wish to travel toward the north and will fill up the carriage, you see."

"Oh?" Jane smiled, "So there is a possibility of six strangers travelling in one carriage?"

The man nodded and turned away to conduct his other duties. Then a young woman approached the man, obviously inquiring about a ticket for herself.

Jane walked toward the bench indicated as the waiting area and muttered to herself, "how cozy. Six strangers."

Jane took out the last letter sent by Silversmith, which summoned Jane on this adventure. Silversmith and Billy Dawes had made progress in their hunt for a woman who could introduce Jane to Benjamin Franklin. Although it occurred in a manner they did not quite expect. Details would be supplied once Jane arrived.

Jane wondered how she would pose this request to Benjamin Franklin. How could she say plainly that she believed her Uncle was trying to halt the enslavement of colonial residents. To honor his memory, she wanted to request that Benjamin Franklin use his political position to put a stop to the cruel practice.

Next, after Mr. Franklin shall have agreed to take on that burden, Jane could put all this behind her and start her life here in the Colonies... if she could still afford it.

Jane slipped Silversmith's letter back into her pocket and was joined by the other young lady who had just purchased a ticket. The young woman sat next to Jane on the bench.

"I believe I'll be travelling with you to Meeting Town," the young woman announced to Jane.

"Ah, fine," Jane replied politely as she clutched her tapestry cosmetics bag on her lap wondering if she had enough in her little bag to allow her to spend the night comfortably at an inn.

Jane's eye caught a glint. The flash was quite bright and she looked around noting the source was some jewelry worn by the woman sitting next to her. The bright sun made this piece sparkle, drawing attention to its brilliance. Jane looked again and recognized the very brooch the woman wore.

This was the same brooch briefly shown to Jane and Silversmith by a young intruder who sought temporary sanctuary in Jane's rooms at Lady Sarah Wilson's estate.

Jane instantly recalled the event.

Silversmith had been getting Jane ready for dinner and for the dramatic performance by the mediocre opera singer, Henry Mossop.

Their preparations were interrupted when a young woman, quite possibly this young lady sitting next to Jane, burst into Jane's bed chambers stating she was reclaiming a brooch Lady Sarah Wilson had stolen from her father, a widower.

In an avalanche of hap-hazard frantic speech, this woman justified her presence by explaining that the specific brooch in question had belonged to her late mother, the woman claimed, and was rightfully hers.

Apparently, the implication was that Lady Sarah Wilson may have picked up mannerisms of a lady, having been engaged in a court some time ago, but had used trickery to fool this young woman's father, duping him and other men into making poor decisions.

This same young woman brazenly scolded Lady Sarah Wilson right beneath Jane's bedroom window. Jane and Silversmith heard the entire incident, yet never mentioned it while they were at the estate.

But, perhaps Jane was mistaken. She looked at the young lady and smiled. The young lady returned the smile. They both sat there in silence for a moment.

"How very peculiar, indeed," Jane accidentally said aloud.

The young lady sitting next to Jane replied, "I beg your pardon? What is peculiar?"

"I beg your pardon," Jane replied, "but you seem rather familiar to me. Perhaps we have met?" Jane offered.

"I don't recall ever being introduced to you, Madame." The young woman stated quite plainly.

"Perhaps we were not formally introduced..." Jane didn't quite know the most polite way to raise this issue, so she thought a moment to devise an alternate plan.

If this was the same girl, then Jane did not want her to think she was a close friend of Lady Sarah Wilson's. This young woman had already quite clearly declared a dislike for Lady Sarah Wilson. Jane also wanted to find out more about Lady Sarah Wilson's past as it might provide more insight onto her own Uncle's story.

Uncharacteristically, Jane opted for a direct approach and turned toward the woman blurting out, "My name is Jane Hargreaves. I've secured a seat on the hired carriage heading north toward Meeting Town. I am rendezvousing with my maid there, as she has arranged for me to meet a wise woman who can give me advice on a personal matter. Where are you headed?"

The young woman replied flatly, "I am also travelling to Meeting Town to discuss matters of business with a woman. Then I will make my journey home to the Carolina colonies." The young woman looked away, bored.

Jane gingerly asked, "May I ask your name? We are, after all, going to be on the same carriage... There is only one carriage heading to Meeting Town today."

Thinking a moment, the woman replied, "Right, then. You did tell me your name was Jane Hargreaves. My name is Eliza Lucas." She paused and turned more fully toward Jane and continued with, "Please don't think me rude. However, the last few weeks have been quite trying and I do plan to sleep on the journey to Meeting Town. So, please do not feel obliged to create polite chatter." The girl, Eliza Lucas, bluntly stated.

"Oh, I'll wager you are from South Carolina? Am I correct? I hear they grow all that nutritious rice..." Jane smiled cautiously.

"Rice! My daddy grows rice! But I also grow Indigo..." The girl actually smiled and Jane sighed in relief, "Miss Hargreaves, was it?"

Jane thought a moment about how to keep this conversation going so she could eventually learn about the hostess at the estate of Lady Sarah Wilson.

Casually, Jane tossed out what she felt was a random fact, "Oh, please call me Jane. The woman I am meeting, Susanna Wright, I'm told is acquainted with that Ambassador, Benjamin Franklin."

The girl, with mouth agape, turned to Jane and exclaimed,

"I am exactly going to see Susanna Wright! She is very clever, indeed, in legal matters... and... medicine. Her father is a doctor... and oh so many things. She is going to help me plan out how to get my indigo plants growing in several fields. We are going to teach others how to grow the crop. So we can start exporting. Soon, you will notice blue will be the fashionable color of this country! We won't need to import inferior inks and dyes from the British Crown, anymore. I shudder to think that they make red, not from pomegranates, but from squashed *Dactylopius coccus*."

"Pardon?" Jane asked.

Eliza added, "Oh, you would probably know it as the Cochineal bug." Jane shook her head and, smiling, shrugged her shoulders.

Eliza explained, "Tiny bugs which cluster on the Opuntia cactus pads...The cactus is a type of plant... until the cacti look as if they are laden with snow, but cannot be because cacti are usually found in warm climates."

Jane replied, "I'm afraid I am unfamiliar with this cactus."

"Well," Eliza Lucas continued, "These bugs collect on the pads or big thick stiff leaves of the plant. Their tiny Cochineal bodies contain an acid, used for warding off predators. But this acid... is a lovely deep red color."

Jane mused, "Interesting chemical mystery."

Eliza replied, "Oh, not a mystery. The chemical components are carbon... um... twenty two parts. Twenty parts of hydrogen and oxygen... a baker's dozen. I mean thirteen parts of oxygen. It melts at 248°Farenheit or 120° Celsius. Indigo, on the other hand, melts at about 734° Fahrenheit or 390° Celsius. Chemically it has the same components. Sixteen parts carbon. Ten parts Hydrogen. Two parts Oxygen, but it also has two parts Nitrogen and makes a wonderful blue color. I think indigo is more versatile as it can be mixed with Carmine to make a purple, but indigo can also be mixed with yellows to make greens. Mix with iron to make a black..."

Jane replied, "It sounds like a rainbow."

Eliza smiled and said, "It is a lovely color on its own, but stunning when mixed with others."

Eliza continued smiling enthusiastically at Jane, "The fun thing about it is when the fabric is in the vat, one may think it has not taken on any color. Then when you pull it out, exposing it to the air, it turns a yellow, then a deeper almost green, then you see the blue appear as if it were magic. You see, cotton will need to be dipped about a dozen times, but silks require about forty dips before the color takes. I had to understand the whole dying process and how the components react to different fibers before I could start experimenting. I first learned all I could about Carmine dyes, you see. Oh, are you familiar with the term carmine dye?"

Jane nodded, "I am. Carmine dye is a deep crimson red. My friend, who is a tailor, buys fabrics dyed with red Carmine dye."

Eliza agreed, "The red dye is held in high regard. Instead of selling it to fabric manufacturers, some dye producers are organizing and talking about trading Carmine dye as a commodity on the London and Amsterdam Commodity Exchanges..."

"They are going to classify a red dye as a commodity?" Jane asked.

"When a good becomes something to sell on an exchange," Eliza explained, "...it simply means that several countries wish to buy this Carmine dye. They don't care who made the dye, but the demand is great... and therefore they can fix the price of the dye sold."

Jane asked, "Doesn't that mean they can artificially raise the price, making the dye only available to the wealthy?"

"I believe," Eliza thoughtfully commented, "that is the direction the red dyes are going. Not there, yet, but if it is true and the dyes do become a commodity on the exchanges, then yes. I think they could set the prices. I think everybody would value a dye cake... so much so, it could become the currency of this country... if we become a country, that is."

She turned, looked at Jane with a serious expression, and lowering her voice, whispered, "That is why I must work with Susanna Wright and hopefully get my technique for growing and processing indigo into everybody's fields. All residents of these colonies can still get high quality dyes and inks. But if they can't afford to buy indigo, they can always grow it themselves... If we cooperate, we could start exporting indigo... or the rice from my father's plantations... and bring money into this land."

"Perhaps one day, your indigo will be so sought after that it also will become a traded commodity," Jane suggested. "How complex is the process?"

Eliza shrugged, "Well, I'm working on perfecting indigo so we can export a quality product. Make a statement to the British Monarchy… and be accessible to all the people here. But developing something of such high quality that we can export it and still make a profit is quite an involved process."

"How involved?" Jane asked.

Eliza answered with, "One must cut off the plant's leaves and place them in a sealed vat of water without air so that it can sit for a day or two. It will make the water bubble. Then, you extract the concentrated liquid into a second tub and try not to faint from the fumes as you paddle it, allowing the sludge to settle to the bottom. Next, you skim off the clear water into a third smaller basin. One tries to avoid disturbing the mud at the bottom of the second tub. The sediment in the second tub is then dried into small bricks or cakes for export shipping. One can discern quality indigo by how the cakes feel light yet hard. The dried bricks should glint in the sunshine. "

Pleased that Eliza Lucas was now enthusiastic about a subject which she obviously cared about, Jane asked, "How very interesting, Eliza. One never thinks about the business, which influences fashions. As I mentioned, I have a tailor friend who has incorporated red into his men's jackets, but when I see him next, I will suggest he promote blue as a fashion. I'm certain he will be quite supportive and want to promote your efforts to develop a profitable exportable product for this country."

Eliza replied, "I've done so much work, yet I feel somehow that some man will swoop in and snatch the credit for my Carolina Indigo. It is simply the way it is, these days."

Jane nodded recalling how her inheritance had been allocated to the nearest male relative.

Changing the subject, Jane smiled and turned to Eliza asking, "And will your husband join you once we reach Meeting Town?"

Jane prodded inquisitively, "Or will he wait for you to return to South Carolina?"

Eliza Lucas replied, "I'm not married," She laughed and said, "As a matter of fact, I was recently cursed by that Sarah Wilson woman who tried to steal this from me."

Eliza pointed to her brooch, "But her curses are meaningless to me. After my business discussions, I must return to South Carolina because my father has entrusted me with managing three estates and several slaves. You see, he is supporting the leadership of George Washington in these battles which surge around us."

Jane mused, "Quite refreshing. It appears that having a woman manage any business here is far more acceptable than it is in England." Jane then abruptly asked, "Is Susanna Wright a successful business woman?"

"Quite successful, indeed," Eliza Lucas replied, then said, "May I inquire, if you are not asking Miss Wright about business, what topic do you plan to discuss?"

"Well," Jane started, "Eliza..." Jane smiled, "um... well... My Uncle, rest his soul, left some work unfinished. To honor his memory, I will request an introduction to Mr. Benjamin Franklin, since he is our ambassador to the Crown, and perhaps encourage Mr. Franklin to write something to... eventually clarify that certain acts must be illegal and punished. "

"Such as property ownership..." Eliza nodded, as if she understood Jane's vague comments.

"Property?" Jane asked

"As you know, in England it is difficult for a married woman to own property. Yet here, where the lands are untamed, women, married or single, can own property as well as businesses. At least in the colonies populated by the Dutch. The ones taken over by the British are conforming to the laws of England. A woman must be careful when selecting a colony to be her home. I plan to stay in these lands and support my father by making the lands we own profitable. There are many hardships in this land, but also many reasons to remain here..." Eliza Lucas explained.

The horses stamped in place. The groomsmen were trying to calm them. Jane wondered what undetectable event transpired to cause these steeds to become suddenly nervous.

Jane looked up. The weather was fine. There was no sign of an impending storm... or at least not one Jane could discern.

Jane closed her eyes and took a deep cool breath, inhaling the scents of horse hair, leather polish, and dry dirt. She heard the footsteps of the people of this busy village going about their daily routines. Then there came to Jane the familiar mixture of ingredients she had seen staff used for polishing hardware: cooked tomatoes, lemon juice, vinegar from the cider of apples, salt and flour to thicken it all. Finally, Jane detected the smoke of burning tobacco from a passing pipe.

Jane opened her eyes.

An opportunity was presented to Jane by meeting this Eliza Lucas. They were both taking the same carriage to Meeting Town and both were scheduled to meet a Miss Susanna Wright.

Plus, this Eliza Lucas was the same one who had burst into Jane's bed chambers as Silversmith was readying Jane for dinner at the Wilson estate.

Jane had to decide if she was going to boldly grab this opportunity or continue with polite banal conversations.

She turned to Eliza Lucas and said quite directly, "May I ask," Jane prodded cautiously, carefully selecting her words, "about that delightful brooch you are wearing? It seems rather an older classical style. Would there be... perhaps... a story you'd like to share as we pass the time while waiting for the other passengers to arrive?"

6 CHAPTER 86: (MAY 1776) Reading The Diary- What to Share with Magistrate

Having just stoked the fire to boil another kettle of water, Witherspoon, the Hargreaves' Butler, refilled the cup of Mr. Bryce Aiden Tyler the partner of Jane's deceased Uncle Floyd. Witherspoon drained the last of the steeped tea from the previous teapot. He poured the liquid through a tiny metal strainer, tapped the strainer against the rim of the teacup, and deposited the tea leaves into a small refuse bowl.

As usual, Mr. Tyler insisted Witherspoon join him for a cup of tea. Witherspoon found this practice quite unusual and awkward, however they were both embarking on an unusual investigation and both required the wakeful effects of freshly brewed black tea. Perhaps unusual practices were apt during unusual times.

"I don't recall details of the day on which Mr. Hargreaves was found dead in his study, Mr. Tyler. I do note, however, hourly events in my daily book. I would need to fetch it... " Witherspoon offered and once he got the nod of agreement from Mr. Tyler, Witherspoon retrieved his daily book.

Witherspoon flipped through the pages and said, "Ah, yes, Mr. Tyler, that day Mr. Hargreaves had given me an unexpected day off. I had gone into town to see a travelling group of performers with..."

"Yes, Witherspoon?" Mr. Tyler smiled, "Was it with somebody in this household?"

"Um. No, sir," Witherspoon replied, "I have a friend employed as kitchen staff in the household of the grand estate down the way. We spent the day together and I did not return until after supper."

So as to avoid embarrassing Witherspoon by noting he had a particular lady friend, Bryce Aiden Tyler simply continued to read the diary and address the task at hand.

"Then," Bryce Aiden Tyler started, "According to Floyd's diary, on the day you read from your daily book, you were out with your lady friend. It appears my secretive business partner had met with an Indian medicine man. Odd that he describes the man instead of using his name. A tall fellow. Perfect English, apparently," Bryce put the book down.

"Does it mention, Mr. Tyler," Witherspoon started, "why he met with this medicine man?"

Bryce Aiden Tyler took a sip of hot tea then looked at Floyd Hargreaves' diary again. "Something about tribes being blamed for the sins of European business men."

"Sins, Sir? Rather dramatic term," Witherspoon commented.

Still studying the pages, Bryce Aiden Tyler shared, "Something here about the profitability of Colonists because they usually have a skill, which increases their price at market."

"What sorts of goods were sold to the Colonists, Sir?" Witherspoon asked as he handed Bryce Aiden Tyler a tea biscuit.

"No, Witherspoon," Bryce Aiden corrected absentmindedly, "not to sell to them... but to sell them... as a slave... for a large profit... So, that is what Floyd Hargreaves was trying to stop."

"The slave markets, sir?" Witherspoon asked.

"No. Trying to stop all of slavery would be nearly impossible. Floyd Hargreaves was trying to stop the kidnapping of colonial residents to be sold as slaves. Perhaps the reason some colonists were seized was if they spoke out against the King. Perhaps they were taken if they possessed a marketable skill. Or perhaps they were just taken to fetch a higher price at market. It matters not. What matters is that some people were ignoring basic civility toward their fellow colonists and selling them!"

"But how would they get them to a slave market? Would not neighbors prevent such displays if the King's men were seen to be marching the roads of each village to whisk away colonial men, women and children?"

"Not," Bryce started still looking at the pages, "not if these men of business had hired local Indians to conduct the actual taking or kidnapping of the European inventory. Perhaps that is why Floyd Hargreaves met with that tall medicine man."

"And if those men of business found out, then that would indeed be impetus for murdering Mr. Hargreaves," Witherspoon added.

Looking him straight in the eye, Bryce Aiden Tyler stated, "Very insightful, Witherspoon. Yes. I believe we have stumbled upon a key motive for the murder of my dear friend and business partner, Floyd Hargreaves. May he rest in peace."

He put the book down and looked at Witherspoon. Took a biscuit and popped the entire thing into his mouth. Bryce Aiden Tyler wrinkled his brow and then frowned at Witherspoon.

"We have, therefore," Witherspoon commented, "a possible method of how the murder was done and where it was committed. We know when the murder occurred. Now we have why the murder was done. Next, we only need to discern who committed this foul deed."

"Yes," Bryce Aiden Tyler concurred, "How, Why, When, Where. We only need the... who..."

"Perhaps, sir," Witherspoon offered, "a man who is intoxicated by the allure of wealth or the glory of working for royalty. A man who does not heed the integrity of conscience and does not know right from wrong..."

Bryce commented, "If Jane is trying to meet Benjamin Franklin and there really is a band slave traders who kidnap European colonists... slave traders who are both secretly supported by the crown to kidnap opponents to the crown and willing to kill to keep it all a secret..."

Witherspoon added, "You may need to be judicious, Sir, about the information you share with the magistrate." Witherspoon then cautioned, "He is paid by the crown."

"Yes," Bryce Aiden started, "but recall you the story of his brother who was wronged by the Crown? That may make him sympathetic to our cause." Bryce Aiden smiled, "If our magistrate had to sell his own brother's lands and send the money back to the crown in England... all for an offense which he still cannot discover... but, you are right. I will be judicious about what information I share and with whom... I cannot risk jeopardizing Jane's life, nor my own."

7 CHAPTER 87: (JUNE 1776) Later At Jane's Hired Carriage

On the wooden bench near the horse carriage rental stand, Jane listened to Eliza Lucas' story about her father, their three rice plantations, and the slaves Eliza managed. Jane also was interested in learning how Eliza knows Susanna Wright, the woman Silversmith and Billy Dawes found through Peter Timothy according to the note Jane received from Silversmith earlier on.

The note Silversmith sent to Jane when Jane was still at Lady Sarah Wilson's Estate, explained that Jane was to meet with a Miss Susanna Wright and request an introduction to Benjamin Franklin.

This conversation was to complete Jane's quest for fulfilling her deceased Uncle Floyd's original plan: eliminate the enslavement of colonial residents.

It would not, Jane mused to herself, reveal who killed Uncle Floyd, but at least she would have done something to honor his memory.

Jane sighed to herself, reasoning that after this, she planned on heading back to her Uncle's home. Jane would need to call for her Uncle Floyd's business partner, Bryce Aiden Tyler and find out the state of their finances to determine if she and Silversmith could continue living in her deceased uncle's house.

With this cacophony of thoughts, Jane suddenly turned her attentions to her new friend, Eliza Lucas, who was continuing with her story as Jane patiently listened.

Jane, then gently prodded her new friend, Eliza Lucas, for information on Lady Sarah Wilson. Eliza had, after all, formed an opinion on this woman who had hosted the opera singer, Henry Mossop. Eliza did, after all, burst into Jane's bed chambers at the estate. Eliza had indeed a very loud interchange with the Lady Sarah Wilson directly beneath Jane's bedroom window as Eliza accused her ladyship of being a fraud and deceiver of men.

Eliza was very clear that the brooch she reclaimed from the estate was bequeathed to her by her dead mother. Lady Sarah Wilson had no right to steal it from Eliza's vulnerable father. Eliza, Jane surmised, was indeed a young woman of great determination and possessed a very clear vision of what was right and wrong.

Jane asked, "Could you share, Eliza, a little about her? You see, I do not know anything of Lady Sarah Wilson's history. I only know she invited my Uncle Floyd and I showed up in his stead."

Eliza replied, "Sarah Wilson... I refuse to acknowledge she has the title of 'Lady' because she does not... At any rate, Sarah Wilson befriended wealthy people who were easily convinced by the impression that Sarah Wilson was royalty. She claimed she was doing the bidding of the British government and she would offer positions of importance in exchange for money or information to use against somebody else. It worked for a while, but then we became aware of her deceptions."

"How was it she was able to deceive so many?" Jane asked.

"She is a practiced liar who believes her own tales," Eliza stated bluntly. "She was able to befriend people easily and always had some story to echo one of theirs so as to build affinity. A common interest or tale of woe. My father is an intelligent brave man, but he found her to be too captivating to use any sane judgment."

Jane asked, "Did not people talk with each other and compare their experiences with this Sarah?"

Eliza replied, "Sarah Wilson used many names, and she is not titled at all, but she would flatter her victims as she took from them ever so slowly."

Eliza sniffed with distain at the thought of Miss Wilson's vile acts, "They never noticed the thieving or unfilled empty broken promises until she had already departed without a new address from which she could be located. I suspect she finally used the name Sarah Wilson, her name given at birth, because it is a name quite plain and simple."

Eliza shook her head annoyed. "Nobody would associate it with deception. But a cheat and liar by any other name... is still a cheat and a liar..."

Finally, Jane remarked, "Indeed. Just as true today as was in Shakespeare's time when he penned Romeo and Juliet: 'a rose by any other name is ...' "

Eliza interrupted, "Yes. Act two, scene two. Yes. I know. However, Sarah Wilson is not one who smells as sweet as a rose, is she? Her smell is quite offensive and pungent once her façade of sincerity is ripped away. That is why I am so very particular about people telling me the truth."

"Indeed you should be," Jane replied then quickly added, "I know where I met you before today, Eliza"

"Oh?" Eliza Lucas started, "Where?"

Smiling, Jane felt she had to bring it up because if she neglected to and Eliza Lucas met Silversmith, it would not appear seemly should Silversmith unknowingly blurted out that she recognized Eliza.

Jane said, "I believe my maid was dressing me before dinner and you surprised us by seeking refuge in my chambers for a brief moment. At Lady Sarah... oh, I mean, Sarah Wilson's estate."

"Ah!" Eliza coughed. "I sought solace in a few rooms... I was single mindedly concentrating on finding my mother's heirloom brooch and then proceeded to escape."

Eliza continued to explain, "I had little time to be properly introduced to the many individuals I encountered. I warned all who would listen. This is why I pleaded my case before they all came rushing to defend Sarah Wilson's non-existent honor by trying to stop me. You understand..."

Jane nodded as she said, "I want you to know that I am not friends with Miss Wilson who, as you say, appointed herself with the title of 'ladyship'."

Jane pondered hesitating if she should share a painful suspicion with this new acquaintance, "I was at the estate because Lady...uh...Miss Wilson had invited my uncle Floyd to an operatic performance, yet my uncle died before the event. I came in his stead."

"It wouldn't surprise me," Eliza snapped, "...if she herself possibly killed your Uncle!"

Eliza noted Jane's shocked expression, and immediately gasped, "Oh, Jane, I am so sorry. That was very rude of me to have that tumble from my lips. Allow me to recall my manners. I am so very sorry to hear of your Uncle's recent passing."

"Do you think, in your opinion," Jane asked, trying to catch her breath, "...that a woman of deception, such as Sarah Wilson, could be involved in a greater scheme?"

"How do you mean?" Eliza asked.

"A more organized endeavor which might involve..." Jane started and struggled for words.

"Involve," Eliza completed, "hurting people for a great profit? I think if Sarah Wilson thought it would work, it wouldn't matter to her who was hurt in the process. She's not sentimental. She will, however, act with compassion and tears if that is the persona which will open your purse."

Jane mused to herself, "How troubling to think that you are made a fool by taking pity on a fellow human in distress... It would make one less apt to help out a stranger if the gratitude one receives is to make you, the rescuer, the victim by stealing something from you."

"Is this why you seek the advice of Susanna Wright?" Eliza started, "I hope to purchase some of her fine silk and dye it with my indigo. Then, hopefully we can present it to Queen Charlotte to prove the Colonies can produce quality goods."

She turned to Jane earnestly confiding, "But your concern seems more intriguing."

"My thoughts are still unformed, Eliza," Jane shrugged.

Eliza Lucas had grown impatient. She smiled, excused herself, left the bench she shared with Jane, and approached the ticket man to ask when she could climb aboard the carriage.

Jane remained seated on the bench. Suddenly, Eliza's voice grew loud enough so Jane could overhear.

Eliza Lucas was upset.

"Why!" Eliza Lucas demanded from the ticket man, "If the horses are brushed and bridled... If the carriage is clean... why may I not board?"

The ticket man replied inaudibly.

Eliza Lucas responded to the man's words with a yelp, "But if the others are not here by now, surely we can leave without them. They can take another carriage."

The man shook his head, no.

Jane turned to look down the street and saw something unexpected.

A man and woman approached, heading straight to the carriage station. These could be the remaining passengers. But as these people came closer, Jane noted they were not dressed in the attire she was accustomed to.

The woman, a bit older, was wearing a doe-skin dress and her hair was in two braids.

The man with her was younger with a shock of long, raven colored hair, neatly combed, glinting in the sunshine. This man was quite tall. Both of these wore moccasins. The older woman was soothing the younger taller man and Jane concluded that it must be a mother and son.

Jane thought this sight very perplexing, yet even more shocking was the fact that this man and woman seemed to heading directly for... Jane...

Eliza Lucas was now following the pointed arm of the ticket man, and squinted her eyes. She saw that these were the passengers and they were not European. She became quite agitated.

Exclaiming loudly enough to be purposely overheard, Eliza stormed, "I am not riding with them. This is not the warrior transport carriage! I need to get to Meeting Town alive!"

Jane grabbed her carpet bag, hopped to her feet, picked up her skirts with one hand and clasped her bag in the other. Jane hurried toward Eliza and the ticket man to aid in quieting the girl.

The ticket man tried to sooth Eliza by explaining the people approaching had actually purchased passage on the carriage prior to Eliza and Jane. The ticket man explained it was his duty to honor their tickets.

Eliza had the option of returning her ticket and waiting three days before the next carriage heading North to Meeting Town was available.

The ticket man said that in the transport business, he had to honor the tickets of all people if they paid the full fare... and those two did... obviously did as there they were... still approaching the ticket stand.

Through Eliza's fits and starts, the ticket man explained the woman appeared to be European herself and both were quite polite and gracious in their manner. Eliza, he assured her, was in no physical danger.

Jane stepped in and pulled the young woman aside whispering, "Miss Lucas! Eliza! This is the only carriage for hire from here to Meeting Town. I checked. We must share. Could you not, perhaps, consider sleeping during our journey, as you suggested earlier? Then, you won't need to interact with them if you do not wish it..."

"You mean," Eliza shot back to Jane, "feign sleeping just so they can slit my throat and then scalp me as has been done to neighbors all over the Colonies?"

Jane, aware of the stories and in particular, Polly's situation, sympathized, "We needn't be foolish, but I would wager that if they wanted to slit our throats, they would wait until we arrived, at which point we have a jolly good chance of scrambling away. Hmmm? Nobody wants to ride for hours next to a scalped corpse... It just isn't done these days." Jane smiled.

Eliza, realizing that her behavior was most inappropriate, finally calmed down and agreed to quietly board the carriage.

As Eliza entered first, Jane quickly turned to the woman dressed in native garb and calmly spoke to mother and son, stating, "I've just met Miss Lucas while waiting for the carriage. I truly believe we shall all have a pleasant voyage, don't you agree? My name is Jane. Jane Hargreaves." Jane curtsied, and with a quick efficient polite smile, she also boarded the carriage and got settled. Jane pushed the sides of her skirts into submission so that she could make room for another to sit next to her.

Jane had addressed the woman, but was surprised to hear the man reply in nearly perfect English after Jane had situated herself. Jane actually didn't expect a reply from either one.

"My mother will be travelling back home to Canada," the man explained, "but we may rest an evening or two in Meeting Town, since that is a stop along the way."

"Canada!" Jane said not knowing what else to say, "I've never been to that country. Lovely, I'm sure."

"My name is -Marguerite or Eunice - whichever is easier for you to remember," the older woman nodded with a smile. "And he," she added indicating the man boarding, "Is my son. He goes by TallMan." The woman then smiled at Eliza Lucas and shared, "I have checked my diary and it is not listed to scalp anybody today, so you may feel free to sleep and be assured you will awaken with your hair in place."

Eliza felt her cheeks become hot with embarrassment. She looked at her hands.

"Two names?" Jane asked the older woman.

"Yes," Eunice replied, "One was the name my parents gave to me, and the other is my Catholic name which I took after I joined the tribe." Her son, TallMan, sat quietly next to her.

"You're catholic?" Eliza Lucas uttered in surprise, "I thought you had all sorts of gods you worshiped."

"I am Catholic. One God and His Son, Jesus died upon the cross to pay for our sins and rose again. Quite normal and sane... and now we are rather drowsy, my son TallMan and I. If you will pardon me I will now sleep," Eunice clarified as she leaned her head back and closed her eyes.

Jane wondered if this woman, Eunice, was weary of dealing with people who assumed her to be a dangerous threat based on her appearance alone.

Following her lead, her son, TallMan, also closed his eyes and leaned his head back.

The carriage driver snapped a whip and yelled, "Eihaa!".

With a jerk, the carriage moved, wheels crunching along the dusty road.

Eliza whispered to Jane, "I don't trust them."

Jane whispered back, "I suspect you didn't trust me when we first met, either..."

Unblinking, young Eliza Lucas clenched her jaw and clutched her coin purse a bit tighter. Clearly, Miss Lucas was unhappy with this travelling situation, but prepared to endure it.

To distract Eliza Lucas, Jane mentioned softly to Eliza, "I think it would be delightful if this country could grow blue indigo so that we no longer have to import it... Imagine all the King's soldiers wearing blue instead of red coats."

Eliza smiled and relaxed a bit, saying, "This country would be self-reliant if we could make what we need here and halt imports to this country."

"Yes. It takes all sorts of different people to come together and create something better, doesn't it?" Jane mused, then indicated their resting companions and said to Eliza, "We should also sleep at bit, as they are. It will be a long journey and I believe we are all quite safe." Jane closed her eyes.

All was quiet save the clip clop of the horses hooves and the occasional scrape of a branch against the Carriage walls. The four carriage occupants were lulled to sleep with the rhythmic sway of the carriage, reminiscent of a baby's cradle. All apprehensions inside the carriage seemed to melt away.

Jane smiled and unknowingly gently fell asleep. Some time must have passed.

Jane awoke startled by a sudden BANG .

Did the other occupants hear it, or was it something she had dreamt?

8 What Just Happened?

Mrs. Dunlap shares the contents of a letter with Polly.

While Silversmith, Jane's lady's maid, is interpreting the actions of the stable boys, she finds out later that kind mistress Jane is now missing. Meanwhile at the secret Meeting Town barn gathering, Button decides he will speak what is in his heart. He does and gets an unexpected reaction and interruption, which just may have saved his life... again.

Back at Uncle Floyd's home, Bryce Aiden Tyler, Jane's Uncle Floyd's business partner, now debates what elements from Uncle Floyd's diary can he share with the magistrate .

And Jane, exploring options to hunt down the elusive truth, brings her across a rocky path of new acquaintances and danger during a bumpy carriage ride. Jane succumbs to exhaustion and falls asleep among these strangers only to be startled awake by an unexpected situation.

9 Did You Know...

Hannah Duston was caught in a raid a century ago. Eunice Williams Marguerite Kanenstenhawi Arosen was also captured in a raid. Both were real women. Their portrayal in this story is fictional and based on true events which occurred in real life. TallMan is a composite character and is not based on one single person. Eliza Lucas was based on a real figure from history.

The German which Polly speaks at the end of Chapter 1 (page 18) *"Wenn es im Lauf menschlicher Gegebenheiten für ein Volk nöthig wird die Politische Bande, wodurch es mit einem andern verknüpft gewesen, zu trennen, und unter den Mächten der Erden...."* is the preamble to the *Declaration of Independence*. The English translation is as follows:

"If, in the course of human events, it becomes necessary for a people to separate the political ties that have linked it to another, and under the powers of the earth....".

The *Firebrand* story references Peyton Randolph who wrote a letter in October 1774. His letter did not unify any of the colonies. Some felt the effort made no difference and they should not go through the struggle of unifying the colonies to resist a King. They felt discouraged from past defeats.

Eventually the colonies did persevere. The nature of our country, the United States of America, has served as a role model for other countries world wide. The lesson should be to continue to support an honorable cause as one day it might just change the world.

10 Vocabulary

In the early 1770s, before the colonies united into the United States of America, some words and terms were used, which may be explained in this section.

Dactylopius coccus (p 70) Today we may reference this bug as the cochineal. It had been used to give the British military coats it's red color. Some say that these bugs will cluster on Opuntia cactus pads. There had been discussions in the colonies that if ever they were going to form a militia, they would not use the red color as the British had done, they would need to find another substance specific to their land. Indeed, they may have settled on the deep blue of Indigo, which is from a plant. Starting on page 71, Eliza explains how she makes Indigo dye.

Posthumously (p23) This is an action which occurred after one has died....

Unobtrusive: Not noticed. Quiet. Shy.

Vexing (p38) means to frustrate to the point of being distressingly annoying or worrisome to that person.

ABOUT Wynter Sommers

Wynter Sommers is the pseudonym for an American writing team, which harnesses multiple skills in technology, research, history and education. Formally trained with a PhD in Education, Wynter Sommers blends academic classroom experience, with corporate sophistication, and a passion for developing more effective student insights through engaging storytelling.

Wynter Sommers has a heart to inspire creativity and develop critical thinking skills, all to encourage readers to make wise choices in life.

Wynter Sommers takes each story and weaves the plot with classic gripping elements, which endure throughout repeated readings, revealing new meanings each time the story is explored. The small choices a reader makes in real life could have a lasting effect in future generations. This set of stories shows the origin of not just Bjorn Esterday and Sarah Paradise, but of their ancestors and the sort of world which was established, which unfolded in each generation until Bjorn and Sarah met.

It is rewarding to learn of heartfelt, thought provoking conversations taking place globally about the characters of these books. Should the reader be presented with extraordinary circumstances, it is the sincerest wish that they act with honor, truth and integrity to overcome obstacles in real life whilst the reader hones skills of self-reliance and collaborative teamwork despite barriers outside of the reader's control. Wynter Sommers hopes you enjoy the other **Bjorn Esterday Was not Born Yesterday** stories in this series.